SWEENEY TODD

-

THE DEMON BARBER

BY

THOMAS PREST

British Library Cataloguing-in-Publication Data
A catalogue record for this book is available from the
British Library

CONTENTS

THOMAS PREST

Thomas Peckett Prest was born in 1810. Originally a talented musician and composer, Prest made a name for himself as a highly prolific producer of 'penny dreadfuls'–a Victorian era publishing trend of lurid and sensationalist stories printed over a series of weeks on cheap pulp paper. His most famous co-creation was the 'demon barber' Sweeney Todd, made famous by the story originally titled *The String of Pearls*. He is also thought to be the possible of author of *Varney the Vampire*. Prest died in 1859.

THE DEMON BARBER

I

Near Temple Bar, at the end of Fleet Street, there stood, in the days of George II, a barber's establishment which was conducted by a man named Sweeney Todd. Its outward appearance would compare very unfavourably with any similar institution of the present day, which may also be said of most other businesses of that period, for shopkeepers merely hung out their signs and made little or no pretence of displaying their wares.

But Sweeney Todd's shop presented a mean, dirty, repulsive appearance, for in keeping with the custom of his profession he practised the minor arts of surgery, such as bleeding, and pulling out teeth; so, in addition to the particoloured pole projecting from the door, there was at the lower part of the window a row of porringers of pewter and blue and white delf, filled with coagulated blood; while some of the upper panes were adorned with a fanciful arrangement of rotten teeth; and as he united to his vocation the art of dressing and renovating wigs, he added the sign of a grizzly old peruke stuck on a wooden featureless block.

The unpleasant aspect of the exterior was well borne out by the dinginess that prevailed inside, where all the paraphernalia hinted at in the window was to be found in the frowsiest profusion.

At a bench within the shop stood Sweeney Todd dressing a wig, with his apprentice close at hand, timidly watching his movements. He was not a pleasant-looking man, this barber; his brows were low and sullen, his cheekbones high, his nose short and pugnacious, and his hard mouth and square jaw suggested brutal selfishness, which was encouraged by his powerful physique.

'Tobias Wragg,' growled Sweeney, without shifting his eyes from his work, 'you're a lucky dog! Don't you think you're a lucky dog to be here learning an honourable and lucrative profession under such a kind and respected master as myself? Eh?' A pause. 'Haven't you got a tongue?' Sweeney turned and scowled.

'Y'yes, sir,' trembled the boy, painfully uncertain as to what his master expected of him.

'Listen to me seriously, Tobias,' said Sweeney with emphasis, 'you are now my apprentice, bound to me body and soul until you are twenty-one. If you attend to business and merit my approval you may have a comfortable and profitable time with me—I shall not tell you what I expect from you, but I shall watch you, and if you turn out the sort of lad I hope, you will have nothing to complain of, and you may be a rich man some day; but, understand this, if you don't do what I require, if you go against me in any way, if you notice things that are not intended for you to notice, or if you talk outside of anything that takes place here, I'll slit your throat as sure as you are alive. Do you hear, you lout?'

The poor boy, greatly alarmed, was about to give an assurance that he would always do his best to please, when the door was opened and a young man attired in nautical style, and bearing on his good-looking face the bronze of tropical skies, entered the shop. This was Mark Ingestre, whose fate closely concerns this story. Sweeney turned from his work and scrutinised his visitor whilst awaiting his commands.

'Good day to you, Mr Barber, may I trouble you to shave me?' said he.

'Why, of course, you may,' answered Sweeney, 'and I venture to remark that I have rarely shaved a face so gloriously tanned as yours. I presume you have been sailing under sunny skies?'

'Yes, I have known what a hot sun is; but I went to the East for a purpose, determined not to return until it was accomplished. And now I am back again in dear old London with my first great object achieved, and the rest soon will be. But I am in haste to visit my dearest friend, and perhaps you can assist me. I find that Mr Oakley, the spectacle maker, has left Fleet Street—do you know his present address?'

'I do, sir,' replied Sweeney. 'He now lives in Fore Street, and outside you will see the big pair of spectacles that adorned his shop in Fleet Street. Sit down, sir—this chair, please.'

Sweeney always tried to learn as much as possible concerning his patrons, so while he prepared to commence operations he remarked that he had heard much of the wealth of the Indies, but those he knew who had been there had but little to show for their toil. He hoped his visitor had fared better.

'I admit that for a long time I had no luck,' said Mark, 'but when a man can show a packet like this he has little to complain of.' As he spoke he produced a beautifully wrought gold casket. Sweeney was all attention.

'That's wonderfully fine,' he said.

'But not so fine as the contents. Look!' said Mark, opening the box and displaying some magnificent pearls. Sweeney's little eyes glittered.

'I don't know anything about pearls, but they look grand. I shouldn't think you'd take less than a hundred pounds for them.'

'A hundred pounds!' laughed Mark, 'why they are worth £12,000.'

'Really! Well, I'm proud of the honour of shaving you,' said the barber. 'Tobias, go to Mr Crick, in Butcher Row, and ask him if he can oblige me with change for a guinea.'

'I can accommodate you with that,' remarked Mark, putting his hand into his pocket.

'Many thanks,' smiled Todd, 'but it is not so much the change I require as a little outstanding matter which I hope the appearance of my apprentice may bring to his mind.'

He followed Tobias to the door as if to give him further instructions, but his object was to put on the catch. Then, having rapidly lathered Mark's chin, he took a few deliberate steps towards a large cupboard, which he opened, and keeping his eyes on his visitor, who lay with his head back waiting for the shaving to commence, Todd inserted his arm and grasped a lever: there followed a swift, soft, churning sound, the floor opened, and the chair with its burden disappeared. In a few seconds *the chair rose empty.*

Sweeney closed the cupboard, scattered sawdust where it had been disturbed, and picked up the casket. 'Just as well that didn't go with him,' he muttered, as he raised the catch on the door, 'although I shall have to see what else he has got shortly. It is well I waited for this, although I am rich enough without it, and prudence prompts me to get away before my greed of gold proves my undoing.'

Tobias returned at this moment, and so quietly that he startled Sweeney, who hastily thrusting the casket under his apron, turned furiously upon his unfortunate apprentice demanding to know what he meant by creeping back like a spy. He answered that he was afraid of disturbing him in the act of shaving somebody. Unfortunately he saw Mark's hat and stick, and thoughtlessly called Sweeney's attention to them, which infuriated him beyond measure, and he was about to rush at the boy when a negro's head appeared in the doorway.

'Well, Satan, what do you want?' roared Todd.

'Massa Ingestre, where he be?'

'How should I know where he is? Who is he?'

'He came here for shave. I wait for him outside.'

'Well, he's gone, and you go after him.'

'He not gone. I wait outside all time.'

It took Sweeney all his time to get rid of the black, and he was much rattled about it, for he felt there was danger in store for him. Many remarks had been made about mysterious disappearances during the past few months, and many enquiries had been made at his shop by friends of the missing ones, who were stated to have set out intending to call at the barber's, and in consequence he was greatly agitated, for he felt that Tobias had only to mention the hat, stick, and casket, to provide a rope for his neck.

'Yes,' he muttered, 'I'll get away as soon as I can, without a word to anyone.'

But avarice held him in a grip, and while he planned a disappearance he was considering how to dispose of the pearls. Sounds of a brawl in the street reached him, but he was too depressed to seek the reason. The door opened, and amid jeers and shouts, a gentleman entered the shop. Sweeney could hardly believe his eyes—here was the very man to help him out of his first perplexity, Mr Parmine, the eminent goldsmith and jeweller.

'Good evening, Mr Todd,' he said, 'I have been molested unfortunately in the street just now, my hat was knocked off and my wig snatched, but although I recovered it there is too much mud on it for comfort, so please do your best to set it right.'

Sweeney was thinking hard. He realised that Tobias was in the way. 'Tobias, you can go home, and see that you are early in the morning.' He followed Tobias to the door, and quietly released the catch.

While he endeavoured to restore the outraged glory of the wig Todd spoke casually about precious stones in order that he might lead to the sale of the pearls. Mr Parmine remarked that precious stones were in no demand, the only things asked for being pearls.

'I have some pearls that I might dispose of,' said Sweeney; 'would you care to buy them?'

'Where are they?' asked Mr Parmine.

'Here,' and Sweeney handed him the casket looking keenly at his face to read his thoughts. Mr Parmine was a jeweller of experience, but with all his self-control he did not entirely conceal his surprise.

'H'm. They look well, don't they? Wonderful how cleverly they get up these imitations! The box is not bad either. What do you think of £50 for the lot?'

'I would rather not tell you what I think,' said Sweeney, striving to keep his temper. 'Hand them over!'

'Well, now I come to look at them a little closer, I think, perhaps, I might be able to manage a little more. Shall we say £100?'

'No,' said Todd savagely. 'I know what their value is and so do you.'

'What do you think they are worth then?'

'Twelve thousand pounds, and I am willing to sell them to you so that you can make a substantial profit, but I want no nonsense or haggling.'

'Well, if they are genuine–I didn't think they were–I daresay I can find a purchaser for £11,000; if so I will advance £8,000.'

'That will satisfy me. I will call tomorrow morning for the money.'

'I am afraid I shall not be able to let you have it—there are important matters to be considered first. A string of valuable pearls cannot be bought like common trinkets; the vendor must give every satisfaction as to how he came by them.'

'And who, may I enquire, will question a man of your standing in the trade?' asked Sweeney, trying to be calm.

'That is not the point; if I give you a large sum for an article I am entitled to know how it came into your possession as a safeguard against possible future complications.'

'That is to say that you don't care how I came to possess the property provided I sell it to you at a thief's price, but if I want its real value you mean to be particular.'

'For a man in your position to possess a £12,000 string of pearls requires explanation and I insist that it is given before a magistrate. Come!'

Mr Parmine, casket in hand, turned towards the door, but as he did so Sweeney sprang upon him with the howl of a fiend. The suddenness of the attack, and the blind fury with which it was delivered, gave him an advantage, and he forced the jeweller towards the fatal chair, intending to strangle him in it, for he could not hold him there and manipulate the lever; but scarcely had he thrown him in the chair than the trapdoor opened without assistance, and Sweeney was only just able to save himself from disappearing with his victim.

Sweeney was terribly alarmed at his narrow escape, and his blood ran cold when he contemplated the failure of his trap. He kicked the casket on the floor and cursed it. What was he to do now! He dare not allow anyone in the shop with the trap exposed, for there was another chair on the underneath side, which rose as the other descended. If the shop were closed the authorities, with so many rumours afloat, were sure to investigate matters. For some time he sat on a *safe* chair utterly bewildered. He was not addicted to strong liquors, but eventually he rose, and going to his parlour, drank several glasses of brandy in succession.

II

The abode of Mr Oakley in Fore Street has no counterpart in the City today; it was one of those picturesque old houses with small windows and quaint architecture which are dear to all artists; in front the small garden, bright with flowers, did not destroy the commercial aspect denoted by the huge pair of spectacles over the door although the workshop was in the rear.

Soon after the events we have just narrated, a military-looking man in a cloak arrived at the gate, and taking hesitating steps up the pathway, he paused in uncertainty. From the parlour window Johanna Oakley watched the stranger, and thinking she might solve his difficulty, she went out and asked if she could assist him. Her beauty and deep melancholy made an instant impression on him, and he enquired if she was Miss Oakley.

'Yes,' she replied, turning a shade paler, 'tell me, have you come about Mark? You look serious–don't tell me any evil has befallen him. He was to have been here three days ago, but he never came. Have you come from him?'

'I have not come from him, Miss Oakley. I am Colonel Jefferey, his friend; and knowing that this was his destination, and that he carried articles of great value–for he returned from India an affluent man–I have come to tell you all I know of his movements, and consider with you what steps

13

should be taken to trace him. After leaving the ship in the river he went with his black servant to a barber's in Fleet Street. His man waited outside, but he never saw his master again. The barber told him Mark had gone, but the man says that is impossible.'

'Hush! Here comes my mother,' said Johanna, 'she had better not see you yet. Conceal yourself behind this curtain.'

Mr Oakley entered with his wife, who, noticing her daughter's distressed appearance, exclaimed, 'Why, child, how pale and ill you look. I must positively speak to Dr Lupin about you.'

'Dr Lupin may be all very well as a parson,' remarked Mr Oakley, 'but I don't see what he can have to do with Johanna looking pale.'

'A pious man takes an interest in everything and everybody,' his wife replied.

'Then he must be the most intolerable bore in existence, and I don't wonder at his being kicked out of people's houses.'

'If the good man has been kicked he glories in it. You would like to see him murdered on account of his holiness, but you won't say as much when he comes to tea this afternoon.'

'What!' exclaimed her husband, 'haven't I told you a hundred times I won't have him in my house?'

'And haven't I told you twice that number that he shall come to tea? I've asked him and he is coming.'

'But, my dear–'

'It's no use your talking. Oh, dear!' she gasped, 'you have brought on a palpitation–you always do. I must have some brandy.'

'Poor girl,' thought Mr Oakley, as he followed her from the room, 'she has been a good wife, although she has changed of late. I ought to be more considerate.'

Colonel Jefferey reappeared at Johanna's behest, and with a sad heart she heard the story of Mark's adventures, and his disappearance whilst on his way to present her with the pearls.

She cared nothing for the pearls, she said; she would rather have Mark than all the pearls in the world, and in order to learn how the Colonel's efforts progressed she agreed to meet him in Temple Gardens that day week at six o'clock if nothing transpired previously.

As he was about to depart, Johanna exclaimed, 'Dr Lupin! How unfortunate!' and the Colonel again retired behind the curtain.

'Yes, maiden,' said Lupin, 'I am that chosen vessel whom the profane call "Mealy Mouth". I come hither at the bidding of thy respected mother to partake of a vain mixture which rejoiceth in the name of tea.'

'Allow me to pass, if you please, Dr Lupin.'

'Thou art disrespectful considering the honour intended for thee. Thy mother has intended thee to be my wedded wife,' and the slimy hypocrite approached her with extended arms.

'Hands off, or you'll repent it!' exclaimed Johanna.

He still persisted, and the sound of Miss Oakley's alarm proved too much for Colonel Jefferey's self-control; he rushed from his concealment and belaboured the reverend gentleman with the scabbard of his sword with great heartiness. Then, leaving Dr Lupin roaring, and holding a black eye, he escaped out of the door while Johanna locked it after him.

III

A few doors up Bell Yard, at the end of Fleet Street, there was about this time a noted pie-shop kept by a Mrs Lovett, whose wares were in such request by lawyer's clerks and sundry others that at certain hours the place was positively besieged by crowds of epicures who swore there were no pies like them. Tobias often had a pie there when a customer gave him a tip, but it puzzled him how his master knew of it.

One afternoon a shabbily-dressed young man presented himself in the shop, and before he could say anything, Mrs Lovett told him to go away as she never gave anything to beggars.

'I'm not a beggar, marm,' he said, 'I've been unfortunate and I'm looking out for a situation. I hoped you might be able to give me one.'

'What, a dilapidated creature like you!'

'That's where you're wrong, marm; it's manners not togs that make the gentleman. It ain't long ago that I kept my own vehicle.'

'Indeed!'

'Yes, I had the best barrow of greens that ever came out of Clare Market, but some villain sneaked it, and I haven't recovered—but I shall.'

'According to what I see of you if ever you are prosperous your insolence will be unbearable. But what employment could I give you except pie-making? What do you know of that?'

'Oh, I was with a baker for four months–I could soon learn your ways.'

Mrs Lovett looked thoughtful. 'I have a man already, but if I give you a trial can you furnish me with a character?'

'A character? No one knows me. The baker died, and I lost the rest when I lost my barrow.'

'No one knows you? Well, come tomorrow morning and I'll show you what to do.'

In the morning he arrived, and in answer to Mrs Lovett, said his name was Jarvis Williams. Raising a trap-door behind the shop she pointed to some stone stairs: 'By this passage, Jarvis, we descend to the furnace and the ovens, where I will show you how to make the pies, feed the fires, and make yourself generally useful.'

They descended into the bakehouse, a gloomy cellar of vast dimensions and sepulchral appearance; a fitful glare issued from various low-arched entrances in which an oven was placed, and there was a counter with pies on a tray.

'I suppose I'm to have someone to help me in this situation,' said Jarvis. 'One pair of hands could never do the work of such a place.'

'Aren't you satisfied?'

'Oh, yes, only you spoke about having a man.'

'He has gone to his friends—to some of his oldest friends, who will be glad to see him. So now say the word, and let me know if you have any scruples.'

'No scruples, but one objection. I should like to leave when I please.'

'Make your mind easy on that score,' replied Mrs Lovett, 'I never keep anybody many hours after they are dissatisfied. As long as you are industrious you will get on well, but as soon as you begin to get idle and neglect my orders you will receive a piece of information that may—'

'May what?'

'There is no occasion for it yet, but after a time, when you get well fed you may need it, and then you will go to your old friends. Now I must leave you.'

'What a queer way of talking that woman has,' thought Jarvis, 'she seems to have a double meaning all the time. And what a singular-looking place too—nothing visible but darkness. It would be unbearable if it wasn't for the pies.'

Jarvis was at liberty to help himself to as many as he liked, but circumstances blunted his appetite, and before long he discovered he was a prisoner in the gloomy vault. The ironcased doors above defied all his efforts to escape, and day by day his hopes grew less, until one day he heard strange sounds on the other side of the wall, which he apprehended to be evil. He waited in trepidation as the sounds grew more distinct, and after much suspense a part of the wall gave way, and through the aperture appeared a face–the face of Mr Parmine.

'Who are you?' demanded Jarvis boldly.

'I am the victim of a murderer,' said Mr Parmine, 'and if you are not in league with him you will help me to escape.'

'I should be only too glad to escape myself, for I've been a prisoner for days.'

'Then it's no use my coming in to you, so you had better join me and we will get out somehow. These vaults are no doubt connected with St Dunstan's if we can find its direction.'

'I can tell you that. This is Bell Yard; so turn your back on it and you look towards St Dunstan's.'

'Then come quickly, for I hear footsteps.'

IV

When Sweeney recovered somewhat from his agitation he decided that his only hope of temporary safety depended upon his ability to restore the trap-door to its former condition. He had a certain amount of mechanical skill, but he was handicapped by lack of suitable implements; still he worked at it until far into the night, and although he could not restore its original action, he contrived to fix it so that it would remain rigid under a man's weight.

Then thoroughly exhausted by mental and bodily fatigue, he threw himself upon a couch and slept for some hours. As soon as he was thoroughly awake he arose, and sliding back a panel in the wall he descended many stairs until he reached a vault beneath the trap-door where he expected to find his victims with their brains dashed out. *They were gone!* and not a trace of them to be seen except some blood upon the stones.

Sweeney was aghast—he could only think the worst. Had Mrs Lovett been there?

Mrs Lovett was his mistress and partner in crime, but no one ever saw them together, for his house backed on to hers, and they met by means of mysterious underground passages entirely unknown to the outer world. By a passage known only to himself and his paramour, he made his way towards the pie-shop, and manipulating a secret spring he caused the wall to open like a door, and he entered the bakehouse.

Sweeney had developed a habit of talking to himself: 'I have too many enemies to be safe. I will dispose of them one by one, till no evidence remains against me. My first step must be to stop the tongue of Tobias Wragg. I need not take his life, for that may be of use to me later; but confinement in a lunatic asylum will silence him. Mrs Lovett, too, grows scrupulous and dissatisfied. I've watched her for some time and fear she intends mischief. A little poison when next she visits me may remove any unpleasantness in that direction. Ha! Who–'

Sweeney turned and saw Mrs Lovett at his elbow, and she was in a very bad temper.

'Sweeney Todd!' said Mrs Lovett in a hard voice.

'Well!' replied Sweeney calmly.

'Since I discover that you intend treachery, I demand my share of the plunder this instant–an equal share of the results of our bloodshed.'

'You shall have it,' said Sweeney, with indifference.

'I mean to,' she almost shrieked, 'every penny!'

'Well, all right, be patient. But don't forget that you are greatly in my debt. Remember that I set you up in business– that I taught you the trade secret'–here he drew his fingers significantly across his throat–'I have kept you in clothes–'

'Clothes!'

'Yes, and you have kept all the profits of the pie-shop, and they belong to me—'

'You want to rob me,' she screamed, 'but I will show you that I will have my due'; and suddenly drawing a knife, she said, 'Now, villain, the whole of the wealth that blood has purchased for me, or I'll slaughter you where you stand!'

'Fool! you should know that Sweeney Todd always calculates his chances,' and springing backwards he drew a pistol from his breast and fired, and Mrs Lovett fell.

'Now the furnace can consume the body and destroy the evidence of any guilt,' he muttered as he opened the furnace door and thrust the body into it.

Immediately the deed was done Todd saw that he had precipitated the end, for the swarm of disappointed pie-eaters would certainly cause an enquiry to be made. How long could he remain with safety?

V

During the next few days Todd was away a great deal, and Tobias was left in charge of the shop, with instructions to do the best he could, and keep his tongue under control. One day, whilst alone, he was startled to hear strange sounds in the barber's parlour (which, of course, was locked in his absence), and still more amazed when the face of Jarvis Williams emerged.

'Phew! out at last,' he exclaimed. 'Why, Toby, old chum, just fancy dropping on you. My word, I have had a time. Where's Todd?'

They were old acquaintances, both hailing from Clare Market; so Jarvis imparted to Tobias the story of his adventures, including what he had heard from Mr Parmine, who had endeavoured to escape by way of St Dunstan's, and also that he had witnessed the murder of Mrs Lovett, whose pies were made of human flesh—poor Tobias felt very sick when he heard that. In return, Tobias gave him the story of Mark Ingestre, the hat, stick, casket, and black servant, and was giving other incidents when Sweeney returned.

Master Williams moved towards the door. 'Well?' said Sweeney questionably. 'It's all right,' said Jarvis. 'I came to see if my father was here, but he's gone,' and away he went. Sweeney looked after him doubtingly; then turning to Tobias he demanded what '*that* fellow' wanted, only to receive the same answer.

'Who else has been?'

'Colonel Jefferey and the black servant kept coming.'

'What did you tell them?'

'Nothing, except that you were out, and I didn't know when you would return.'

'Are you sure that was all?'

'Yes; I never said a word about the things left behind, or the gold casket you had.'

'I *had*, villain!' yelled Todd, and in a burst of ungovernable fury he seized a knife and sprang after his apprentice, who dodged round tables and chairs in terror. But Sweeney heard the rattling of a coach on the cobbles cease at his door: he was evidently expecting it, for he put up the knife and opened the door. 'I'll let you off this time—come, we'll go for a ride. Get in,' he said, pointing to the coach; but Tobias, afraid, refused to move, so Todd called the driver, and the boy's chance of dodging was ended.

They rode to a private mad-house at Peckham, kept by a man named Jonas Fogg, with whom Todd had had previous transactions, and who appeared to know what was expected of him. Todd had some conversation with Fogg, explaining that Tobias suffered from delusions, and was liable to make dangerous statements concerning himself, but he hoped that twelve months' treatment in Fogg's humane institution would restore him to reason, and for that period Todd would pay in advance. Having arranged everything, Sweeney departed, while poor Tobias was taken before the master who caused him to be put in a dark cell, and into a strait jacket if he offered any resistance.

While Fogg was rubbing his hands with satisfaction at receiving twelve months' keep for a patient *who might die in two months*, he little thought how this event would terminate.

When Jarvis Williams left Todd's shop he felt uneasy about Tobias, and he hovered near the shop considering. Soon he saw a coach of ominous appearance arrive, and, later, Tobias was bundled into it and it rumbled away.

Londoners of that day were capable pedestrians, having to depend on their legs for the accomplishment of their travels, and Jarvis thought nothing of following the coach to its destination. For some time it crawled, but afterwards the pace mended, and a journey of about four miles saw the end.

When Sweeney came out alone, Jarvis set off at a good speed towards Clare Market, where some of the toughest rascals in London were to be found, and gathering nearly a score of them they started to the rescue of Tobias.

A leisurely journey to Peckham enabled them to arrange plans *en route*.

It was an awkward place to enter without permission–high walls had to be scaled if they could not gain access from the front door, and that had a grating in it through which a porter scrutinised all visitors. Fortunately the names of the establishment and its proprietor were prominently displayed outside, so Jarvis, having arranged his gang in crouching attitudes where they could not been seen from inside, rang the bell.

'What do you want?' said a voice through the grating.

'Mr Sweeney Todd sent me with an urgent message for Mr Fogg, and I would like to see him,' said Jarvis.

After a brief delay and sounds of bolts and chains being withdrawn, the door opened; Jarvis stepped inside and immediately a desperate rush swept the porter off his feet, and, notwithstanding his strength, he was tied up, legs and arms, before he could resist. Fogg, hearing the noise, put his head out of his room, and they swooped down on him, demanding that Tobias should be produced at once. Fogg, although terrified, tried to equivocate, but they handled him so roughly that he shouted for his attendants, and as they appeared, one by one, they were overpowered, and Tobias was released.

The money Todd had paid was lying on the table, and Fogg would have conveyed it to his pocket if a blow on his hand with a cudgel had not interfered with his plans and allowed his visitors to pocket it instead. They successfully hunted for refreshments, and then, after ransacking the place and releasing all the unfortunate inmates, they left Fogg and his satellites bound hand and foot and departed. Their offence was a hanging one in those days, but they felt certain they need not fear Jonas Fogg.

VI

The figures of Adam and Eve on St Dunstan's Church were striking the hour of six when Colonel Jefferey arrived in Temple Gardens to keep his appointment with Johanna Oakley. She was already there, pale and beautiful, and trembling with anxiety. Unfortunately the Colonel could add but little to what she already knew; he could only tell her of several uneventful visits to the barber's, although he was convinced that Todd could unravel the mystery, and he added that he was in communication with an expert crime investigator.

Johanna thanked him in spite of his ill-success, and she looked so lovely in her distress that the Colonel decided in the event of Mark never returning to strain all his energies to make her his own; but he was a man of honour and a true friend, and while there was the slightest hope remaining he would not relax his efforts on her behalf. They walked together to Fleet Street, and as she would not accept his offer to escort her home, they parted opposite Todd's shop. The Colonel was going towards Bow Street when a mysterious voice muttered in his ear, 'You seek news of a missing friend; if you will come with me I may be able to help you,' and turning he saw an individual whose features were concealed by a mask.

'I must first know who and what you are before I consent

to be guided by a man who hides his features behind a mask,' said the Colonel.

'I wear this mask for other purposes than concealment,' said the man, 'but since you distrust me I will leave you and you will remain without the information you desire.'

'Stay, friend, have you no token to prove your sincerity?'

'Yes, and one that will appeal to you,' he replied, at the same time putting the casket of pearls into his hand.

'Good heavens!' he exclaimed, 'This convinces me—where do you wish me to go?'

'To the shop of Sweeney Todd, the barber, where you will learn something that will surprise you.'

The shop, being only a few yards away, was soon reached, and Colonel Jefferey received the surprise he was promised, for the shop was occupied by constables, and the stranger, removing his mask, revealed the malignant features of Sweeney Todd. The barber, pointing to the Colonel said, 'This is the man who murdered Mark Ingestre, and if you search him you will find the casket of pearls in his possession.'

Colonel Jefferey was astounded; but as the constables gathered round he held out the casket.

'There is no necessity for searching. That villain handed them to me in the street just now as a guarantee of good faith, telling me that if I would visit this shop with him the mystery of Mark Ingestre's disappearance would be cleared up. If Mark has been murdered he is the murderer.'

'You may have a satisfactory explanation,' said the leader of the constables, 'but this is a murder charge, and it is my duty to take you before a magistrate.'

'I am quite ready,' said the Colonel.

Sweeney was chuckling to himself over his cleverness, when the officer said, 'You must come as well.'

'Of course,' replied Sweeney, 'but I'll follow on as I have something to do first.'

'You will come now; there is a counter-charge of murder against you.'

'Nonsense!' said Sweeney, 'why, I've handed the murderer over to you. I'll come on as a witness afterwards.'

'Bring him along!'

And Sweeney joined the party with a constable holding each of his arms.

Let us now refer to certain matters that may seem to require explanation. The Church of St Dunstan's (it was pulled down and rebuilt 1831-3) was an ancient affair that stood 30 feet south of the present church, and beneath it there were extensive underground passages and vaults stretching away in various directions, which few people had ever heard of or suspected to exist. Sweeney Todd, by accident, made the discovery, and after many nocturnal explorations, he concluded that they were entirely forgotten, and that it was safe for him to use them for his own purposes.

A conversation with a skilful mechanic gave him the idea of the trap-door, which they made between them, and when it was completed Sweeney tested its efficiency upon the unsuspecting mechanic, and became the sole possessor of the secret. He worked cautiously, murdering many, and grew rich, but the disposal of the bodies troubled him, as he had to bury them beneath the stones underground.

He had been intimate with Mrs Lovett for some time when he discovered that a passage could be made to communicate with a shop in Bell's Yard, and he installed her in it as an expert pie manufacturer. Then the horrible idea occurred to him that it would be both profitable and expedient if she used the flesh of the dead for her pies, and if any of their assistants suspected anything–*they went to their friends.*

At last the mechanism of the death-trap failed, and Mr Parmine escaped, because of its irregular action, instead of throwing him on his head, caused him to turn a somersault and fall on his feet, sustaining only minor injuries.

Sweeney Todd prided himself upon his cunning, but little he dreamt what it would do for him. He expected to be at liberty to depart after giving evidence against Colonel Jefferey, but both were detained until the morning. This was a bitter disappointment to Sweeney, who had everything ready for a flight which, during his frequent absences, he had arranged with the captain of a ship in the Thames, who was to sail about midnight–and time and tide wait for no man.

When they appeared before the magistrate Sweeney had a shock which paralysed him with terror; for there, seated beside the magistrate, was the murdered Mr Parmine, and confronting him were Tobias Wragg, Jarvis Williams, Mark Ingestre's black servant, and the captain of the ship he was to have sailed in. It seemed that constables and watchmen had been keeping an eye on Todd, and he was aware of it; and in order to gain the few hours he required to join the ship he endeavoured to betray Colonel Jefferey, but with a fatal result to himself. Every word that went to clear the Colonel struck a blow at Sweeney, with the result that he was committed for trial at the Old Bailey, while Colonel Jefferey went free.

When the trial opened, Sweeney was staggered to see the murdered Mark Ingestre sitting with Colonel Jefferey, and the effect on his nerves was disastrous. It was stated that Mark would have appeared before, but he was too badly injured to be moved, and that but for the defect in the trap he would have been killed. He owed his escape to Mr Parmine.

The evidence of Mark Ingestre and his black servant, of Tobias Wragg, Jarvis Williams, Mr Parmine, and others was overwhelming, and when the judge pronounced sentence of death Sweeney was in a state of abject collapse, from which he never recovered.

His hanging was a great event, for the public were more bitter against him than any other malefactor on record, and especially violent were those who found themselves unwitting cannibals through his instrumentality, and he was pelted all the way to the gallows, his escort having great difficulty in preventing the mob from tearing him limb from limb.

It is satisfactory to record that Mark and Johanna had a happy time in store, and that Fortune was kind to the others who deserved it. Being parted from his treasure embittered Todd's last hours, but it probably did good elsewhere, for Jarvis Williams appeared abundantly supplied with money, possibly due to his subterranean investigations, and by his instrumentality Tobias and his mother were installed in the pie-shop, which they thereafter conducted in exemplary style.